William Hathaway Forbes

The Poems of William Hathaway Forbes

From 1881 to 1897

William Hathaway Forbes

The Poems of William Hathaway Forbes
From 1881 to 1897

ISBN/EAN: 9783337408039

Printed in Europe, USA, Canada, Australia, Japan

Cover: Foto ©Andreas Hilbeck / pixelio.de

More available books at **www.hansebooks.com**

THE POEMS

of

William Hathaway Forbes

1881 TO 1897

Privately Printed

1898

PREFACE

ALMOST all these verses are impromptu, and were written at the meetings of the Game Club on subjects given out at the moment by the host or hostess. They were never corrected, and were generally forgotten at once by their author, who, when they were brought to his notice months afterward, was often surprised to find his own initials below them, and was interested in them as quite new to him.

E. E. F.

AUGUST, 1898.

CONTENTS

APPENDIX

DREAMS

A RE dreams like birds that only pause to sweep
With lightest touch our eyelids when we sleep?
Or are they waves that take us as they go
To float on ocean depths of joy and woe?
They may be breezes passing in the night
That seem to wake us to a new delight;
They may be clouds, and touched with every hue,
To show us what the painter Sleep can do;
Or prophets of the things that are to be,
Which in the light of day we cannot see,—
They masquerade in every shape in turn,
In magic ways that we can never learn.
Come back, old friends, come back, if still you may,
And help to still this restless nerve of day;
Gild once again those fairy scenes of youth
That always seemed but never could be truth.

January, 1896

CHRISTMAS VERSES

IF thou dost ask me why the summer flew
   Like a bright dream, with all its happy hours,
And Autumn with foreboding silence grew,
Till Winter set its seal upon the flowers,

I say — if Summer had its thousand charms,
A thousand more are waiting for the eyes
That watch when Winter, with its jewelled arms,
Beckons the children to the Christmas prize.

Yet should you push the question home once more,
Does Winter most, or Summer stir the breast?
Give me the happy dream beside the shore,
Let me keep that, and you may have the rest.

27 *December*, 1882

DIFFIDENT

SUBJECT: *Adjectives Drawn by Chance*

WITH my heart in my mouth did I ask her to
dance,
While the horns and the fiddles so merrily played—
(We both of us came to the party by chance!)
I vow that I scarcely could hear what she said.

But she rose from her seat and she gave me a glance,
While the horns and the fiddles so madly they
played;
With my eyes on the floor I caught it by chance,
But I guessed what she meant and I won the
fair maid.

20 March, 1883

11

VULCAN AND VENUS

"YOU well may laugh, who pass the sunny day
   In gleesome dances or in joyous play,
While I with heavy blows a chain must weld
To hold the mightiest giant e'er beheld."

"Laugh on! my work shall stand when love's poor
      game
Shall be no more than a forgotten name,
While all who listened to its mocking voice
Or soon or late repented of the choice."

"Ah, foolish god, not so much lame as blind,
You cannot see the bond that holds mankind!
While skies shall bend over the answering sea,
Love shall be first,—all, all must follow me."

20 *March*, 1883

A ROSE

LOOKING upon a rose I did forget,
  Just for a little moment, all things sad.
Could we but make such moments years! and yet
  Were life all roses would it keep us glad?

20 *February*, 1884

IDEAL OF HAPPINESS

YOUR work done,
  And your neighbors' not!
Yourself cool,
  And your neighbors hot!
Yourself warm,
  And your neighbors cold!
Yourself young,
  And your neighbors old!
Yourself merry,
  And the rest sad!
Yourself good,
  And the rest bad!

20 *December*, 1884

MOTTO FOR A SUN DIAL

I GATHER the hours from the sky,
  And give them to you on earth.
Use with heed! you shall know why
  The mighty world had birth.

29 *April*, 1885

THE AMBITIOUS ICICLE

A N icicle hung on the side of a wall,
   And wanted to go to the Emperor's ball,
For when the sun shone, such a glitter she made
She thought all the diamonds were thrown in the shade,
And she said, " I am slender and taper and tall,
And too debonair to remain on the wall."

An Irish potato lay close to the wall,
And heard the bright icicle talk of the ball;
With envy and pride he was ready to burst,
And he said, " By your lave, I'll be getting there first."
So he put on his jacket and went off to look
How to scrape an acquaintance with Jacob, the cook.
Alas! the poor icicle stuck to the wall:
The potato in triumph appeared at the ball.
The icicle wept to the end of her life—
The potato was waved on the Emperor's knife;
And the last that the icicle heard of the 'tater
Was a half-smothered promise that he'd see her later.

4 *February*, 1885

THE WOOING OF KATE CAMERON
BY ROB FORBES

SEE them with foot upon the heath,
  A slender youth and chieftain gray,
Facing each other, between them death,—
  Which shall with him stay?

On either side the clansmen stand,
  Their brows as black as night;
All know too well whose bloody hand
  By treachery had won the fight

When Cameron's chieftain with his sons
  Sank into night upon the field.
The Cameron's blood too freely runs,
  And the last man refused to yield.

And now the targe is thrown away,
  The lightning blows come fast,
God for the right! We win the day,
  The traitor's down at last.

'T was one for vengeance and one for love
As the broadsword cleft his brain,
And the youth may pass to the hills above
And claim Kate Cameron for his ain.

19 *May*, 1885

NOTE.

According to tradition, there was once a bitter feud between the Camerons and the Muats, which had proved so bloody that finally the chiefs of the two clans agreed to settle the matter in a certain lonely glen with but twelve horse on a side.

The wily and treacherous chief of the Muats brought two men on each horse, and, rather than withdraw from the contest, the Camerons fought in unequal combat, until their old Chief, his three sons, and the rest of his followers were dead. The Chief of the Muats was one of the few survivors on his side.

Rob Forbes, the youngest son of Lord Forbes, fell in love with the beautiful Kate Cameron.

In reply to his entreaties, she met him in the same glen that was the scene of the tragedy, and there told him that she had vowed to marry no man but him who should have killed the mighty Lord of Muat, the murderer of her father and three brothers.

Rob Forbes at once challenged the old Chief, although his clan thought that he was going to certain death.

The fight was long. The enthusiasm and strength of the young man offset the skill and experience of the older, till, finally, seeing an opening, Rob dashed in and buried his dirk in the heart of his foe.

He claimed of her mother the hand of Kate Cameron, and that spirited lady accomplished the wedding before the blood of her foe was dry on the dirk of the victor.

Rob Forbes took for his crest a lifted hand and dagger, with the motto *Non sine causa.* This, as engraved on an old seal with the Forbes arms with bears'

18

beads, is used by the family still. But I have had no success in my attempts to learn why this branch of the family inherited it instead of the motto *Altius ibunt qui ad summa nituntur* with the arms of Lord Pitsligo, from whom they are descended.

Our father, Mr. John M. Forbes, received from the uncle for whom he was named, a seal ring engraved with *Non sine causa* and the arms, but he cannot recall why it is ours rather than the other. When he used it in China in his youth, it was the means of his becoming acquainted with a Scotch Forbes, who recognized it, and, as I believe, had the same crest.

THE REPLY TO A PARTING WISH

A LUCKY dog indeed am I
On all the counts you name.
But one thing more
You did not score
As good as true, —
A poem from you;
And I'm to have that same!
How shall I e'er reply?

A thousand wishes from the East,
A thousand from the West, —
All these for you;
While skies so blue,
And woodland reach,
And shining beach,
Are wooing you to rest.
And, lady, would you feast?

A million bluefish swim the bay;
The lobster lines the shore;
   The eager shrimp,
   The oyster limp,
   The restive clam
   (On which they cram),
And half a hundred more,
All silently await their day.

And when the skies forbid a storm
And you 're inclined to roam,
   Come down the bay
   Some breezy day, —
   The shining wave
   The road shall pave, —
And seek our island home;
Your welcome shall be warm.

May, 1885

"FRIDAY'S BAIRN IS LOVING AND GIVING"

IF he has learned to love and give,
  And yet has learned no more,
That happy youth has gained the day,
Has found the clue that shows the way
  To all the happiness we have in store.

30 *December*, 1885.

CASSANDRA

WHILST thou, O man, with common soul
    Dost live content to know to-day,
I see the coming seasons roll, —
    I see along the gleaming way, —
I tell when passion's heated hour
    Shall end in deeds that quench their fire;
I see the dreaded war-clouds lower,
    The son in combat with the sire.
But thou, O youth, with shining brow,
    And heart with love's fresh memory fanned,
Wouldst thou thy happy future know,
    Seek prophet of some other land.
The gods forbid thee to believe,
    And thus the future I can say
To those alone who seek reprieve,
    Whose future brings an evil day.
Ah, could I for one season brief
    Tell all the world of tidings gay,
And hide these presages of grief,
    Content I'd die that happy day.

27 January, 1886

"LIKE THE CAROL OF BIRDS AT DAWN"

THE architect said to his charming wife
    (Like the carol of birds at dawn),
"Here's a gay bonnet, my love, my life;
    'T is the colour of the fawn."

The lady hummed a little tune
    (Like the carol of birds at dawn),
And said to herself, "Some little boon
    Is the price of that bonnet, I'll be sworn."

The architect whistled a lively air
    (Like the carol of birds at dawn),
"Shall we hie to the theatre, O lady fair,
    "Mikado or Colleen Bawn?"

"O wait till in our new house we wake
    (To the carol of birds at dawn);
Be sure no rest or fun I'll take
    Till the mason and plumber are gone."

"Oh, that reminds me," he warbled low
  (Like the carol of birds at dawn),
"I asked the Game Club to meet there, so
  We must finish the house by Wednesday morn."

The lady gave him a single look
 . (That hushed the carol of birds at dawn),
And the architect his departure took
  With the rapidity of the fawn.

The house was done in about a week
  (Tho' the birds would carol about the dawn),
But the wife and the bonnet and husband meek
  Are going to-night to the Colleen Bawn.

3 *March*, 1886

THE FIRST OF OCTOBER

HE loved his horse and dogs, the hillside fair,
    The forest filled with autumn jewels rare;
He thought himself as free as birds that fly
With gallant wing across the rich blue sky;
And as he rode along the sunny glade
He did not dream his life could have a shade.
But somewhat else had entered his young life;—
Not yet the heritage of martial strife,
Nor mourning sorrow's all too sudden shaft,
Nor warning yet of worldly guile and craft.
Something that day had made his heart beat quick,
And all the air for breathing seemed too thick.
What was it bade the deeper colour rise,
And brought strange fear into the daring eyes?
If thou canst tell me, thou has found the key
To mankind's greatest, fairest mystery.

28 *April*, 1886

AFTER THE FIGHT

WHEN the battle-cloud hung low
  And the air felt thick and hot;
While the musket-roll seemed slow,
  Though the field was quick with shot,

He rode along the wavering line,
  And a bugle-call was in his face,—
"Not to-day shall man of mine
  A single foot give place."

And in his heart was ever a song,
  A song of victory and joy;
His coming made the timid strong,
  Though he looked still a boy.

After the fight the soldiers rest,
  When night's dark veil is drawn,
But the bayonet that stilled his breast
  Has made a nation mourn.

12 *May*, 1886

THE LAUGH OF THE LOON

THE loon swims over the oyster-bed,
　　And cries "Wa-hoo" to the lobster red;
The minnow trembles beneath his tread,
And the sword-fish stands at bay.

The sun is sinking in the west;
Where should he sink? — he does his best.
Is this a proper time for jest?
Wa-ha-ha-hoo, I say.

Wa-hoo! I don't much care how soon
You know that this is the laugh of the loon.
"Wa-ha-ha-hoo," he cries to the moon,
But it does n't do any good.

30 *November*, 1886

HOMESICKNESS

OR

WAS IT FOR ME?

THE train moved out from Washington
  And left its varied spires behind;
And in the chair in front of me
  A charming girl (I am not blind)
Reposed. She held a bunch of flowers,
And evermore the tedious hours
She strove with novels to beguile.
She stopped; she gave a pensive smile —
    Was it for me?

She'd not been much away from home,
  And soon confidingly did talk —
Did the train stop at Baltimore?
  And also at New York?
And as the happy hours rolled on,
She told me of gay Washington,

And spoke of all the people high;
Then from her breast escaped a sigh!—
    Was it for me?

We did not speak of wife at home,
    Three daughters and a son;
It certainly is rather droll
    These matters were not touched upon.
For Byron we were full of praise,
And talked of Scott's romantic lays;
And when, too soon, New York was near,
There dwelt upon her cheek a tear—
    Was it for me?

My voice I scarcely could command —
    I stepped outside for air;
And as I gazed the landscape o'er
    Her face was everywhere.
For she was fair and loved to roam,
But never had been far from home.
My frenzied thoughts I could not tell
Yet I returned to say farewell,

When I beheld — could it be true?
Upon my chair a violet blue —
　　　Was it for me?

Just here we reached a tunnel dark, —
　　The porter must have had a fee,
For not a lamp and not a spark
　　Could show the neighbours her or me.
It was not more than minutes two
Before the train had rattled through;
But as we neared the dark abyss
There hovered on her lips a kiss —
　　　Was it for me?

Whate'er betide my course was clear, —
　　I placed the violet next my heart;
The ferry-boat was coming near,
　　And soon my Boston train would start.
And she was now to meet Papa —
" That can't be he who smiles from far;
The idiot is too young by half!"
Alas! I heard a mocking laugh —
　　　Was it for me?

VERSES

ON THE SUBJECT — THINGS ONE WOULD RATHER HAVE
LEFT UNSAID

W E walked upon the moonlit beach,
    Her hand within my arm;
'T was not the sort of night for speech,
    I thought it was no harm

To give the hand a little squeeze,
    That widow's hand so slender —
This made her upward turn her eyes,
    Her eyes so soft and tender.

She asked me why I pressed her hand;
    I stammered with a pause,
"I — I thought it was my own," and
    She said, "Take it, it is yours."

January, 1889

A FOOTSTEP

THE maid stands alone
  Beside the dark hedge,
Her heart is not still,
  She has given a pledge;
And the setting sun shines
  On her golden hair,
And blue and gold
  Seems all the air;
While the swallows come out
  To their play in the gloaming,
But she does not note
  Their careless roaming.
Her face grows wistful
  As the night falls —
The silent sidewalk
  Her heart appals —
A footstep distant
  Now nearer sounds,
Again the skies glow,
  And her heart bounds.

April, 1887

3   33

FAIRY STORIES
ARLINE AND THE WILL O' THE WISP

MAIDEN fair, why dost thou tarry
    Abroad in the gloaming,
Each night as sunset fades away
    On the mountain roaming?

I like the best the darkening skies
    When the swallows hover;
And I follow the light of my lover's eyes
    The mosses over.

What name does thy lover bear, sweet child?
    Wilt bring me near him?
Why dwells he on the moorland wild?
    Dost thou not fear him?

He is gentle as the evening breeze
    That stirs the river,
And makes soft music in the trees,
    And I fear him never.

His step is light as the thistle-down,
  Or a bubble flying;
And his song is sweet, for 't is all my own,
  Tho' it leaves me sighing.

Only this hour is his alone
  While dews are falling —
"Oh, keep me not, I must be gone,"
  His voice is calling.

30 *November*, 1887

A COMPARISON

E. L. W. TO THE OCEAN

LIKE the tips of the waves as they dance in the
    sun
Is the wit that rides over her billows of fun.
While the ocean at rest, when the storm has gone by,
Has the calm of her heart and the blue of her eye.

28 December, 1887

SUPPOSING EATING AND DRINKING WERE ABOLISHED—WHAT THEN?

THE sun has risen on a glorious day,
　　And man awakes to his emancipation;
Now food and drink no more a part can play,
　　And gone are gluttony and dissipation.

How fresh the air seems, and how bright the sky!
　　Delicious breezes stir the languid bough;
Each drop of dew makes rainbows to the eye;
　　The hours glide by—the loiterer knows not how.

No breakfast-bell in his behalf is ringing,
　　No luncheon-hour can interrupt his joy;
He wanders on in woods where birds are singing,
　　While thoughts ethereal his mind employ.

Now all things eatable may take a rest;
　　Th' unshrinking oyster opens wide his shell,
Views all the charms of ocean with new zest,
　　And ponders many things he may not tell.

The dubious sausage and the blithesome tart
   Recline neglected by the pantry door;
The stormy pancake, rich with native art,
   May stir us up to efforts new no more.

The turkey and the grasshopper now walk
   In close accord, and like each other's looks;
While yonder vessel (judging by their talk)
   Is taking home a cargo of French cooks.

Is it a dream, or is this freedom mine?
   Can I unharmed drink in these careless hours,
And all unchided not return to dine?
   And can my wife have time to arrange her flowers?

Then have we reached millennium in fact;
   We shall ne'er know aught but unclouded days.
My time for work will always be intact,
   While long-due calls my wife all blissful pays.

4 *April*, 1889

ORPHEUS

VERSES SUGGESTED BY CERTAIN LINES OF POETRY

DRAWN BY CHANCE

"ORPHEUS with his lute made trees"
    (I could n't do it should I try).
To lands where rivers never freeze
The following month did Orpheus hie,
But then he did not tarry long,
His garments (partly) with the "purp"
Remained, while he resumed his song
On earth, resolved not to usurp
The business of his friends below,
And ever since that time, you know,
When barking dogs disturb the ranch,
You all might see with greatest ease
Old Orpheus climb his lute-made trees
And hide him in the topmost branch.

28 *December*, 1887

"ON THE BROW OF A HILL A YOUNG SHEPHERDESS SAT"

ON the brow of a hill a young shepherdess sat,
　　While the south wind was sending swift waves
　　　thro' the field.
She was holding a rose: was she wondering what
　　Young Rob wished to say when he gave it and
　　　kneeled?

Not a word had he spoken; his lips were so shy
　　As he passed to the wood where his axe could be
　　　heard,
And perhaps the lad also was wondering why
　　He could think of a thousand but say not a word.

From cloud land long rows of white fleeces passed by,
　　Through the deep woods came out the clear song
　　　of a bird,
And at sundown the maid and the lover so shy
　　Had heard the sweet song and had spoken the
　　　word.

5 December, 1889

APRIL

AMBITIOUS brook
　　From mountain nook,
Now leaping tiny chasms,
And now, with mimic spasms,
Rearing a tawny head
From thy uneasy bed, —
Thou dost through meadows gay
Fearlessly seek thy way,
And mean'st to be a river blue
Before the frolic month is through.

Speak to me, telltale brook,
While in thy face I look.
What wast thou when the year was young?
What didst thou ere the robin sung?
Say, in some prison strong
Have giants held thee long,

Waiting a fairy touch?
Or didst thou suffer much
    Day after day,
    Kept from thy play?

I was a peak of snow
Seen from dim plains below;
    I was an icy dome
Gleaming on mountain head;
Round me the storm king sped,
Sending his tidings dread
    To many a startled home.
Sometimes the breezes mild,
    Cooled by my ice and snow,
Paused by some fevered child
A while to fan its brow
    In the far town below.

Glorious sights were there
Up in the starry air, —
The meteor's flashing ray,
And the near sun by day.

Yet did I long for change
On yon bright mountain range;
And fairy April's welcome touch
O'ercame the winter king's command,
And sent me here with antics gay
Amid thy fields and flowers to play.

23 January, 1890

VERSES

TO THE MUSIC OF A SONG CALLED

"THE SHAMROCK, THE ROSE, AND THE THISTLE"

ONCE more on the air is the scent of the heather,
  As we pass by the hill where the gay thistle
    grows,
And the lass of my heart she is asking me whether
  I love it as well as the shamrock or rose.

And I say to my sweet that the Douglas's daughter
  Knows old Scotland is first in the wide world
    for me;
From the braes of Loch Ness to the waves of Clyde
    water,
  The thistle for aye, by the land or the sea.

15 *September*, 1889

IF ONLY DREAMS WERE TRUE

OH! gentle night,
  Whose sister, loving sleep,
Kisses from weary lids
All cares that blight!
No longer do I weep,
When thy soft magic bids
Fair dreams from wonderland,
Around my couch to stand.
If only dreams were true!
How could we part from you?

If only dreams were true,
The shepherd youth below
Yon mountain 'gainst the blue,
Counting the tedious hours,
Would pass through realms of snow,
And passing, see the towers
Of far-off cities gleam,
As often in his dream.

If only dreams were true,
The knight on yonder plain,
The castle carried and his service done,
Would seek thy bower again,
Fair maid, and find another victory won
From thy sweet eyes so blue.

9 January, 1890

IF I WERE A PRISONER, WHAT WOULD I WRITE ON THE WALL?

IF I were prisoner? That, in sooth, am I,
  O lady fair, till thou wilt set me free;
Yet can I see a prisoner's share of sky,—
  Thine eyes, my love, and heaven enough for me.

My prison walls are not indeed in sight,
  Yet fast they hold me through the changing days;
But could I find them, I would thereon write
  In lines of flame to tell the world thy praise.

And though I wander over pathless seas,
  Or climb far mountains to their summits bare,
'Tis but to find such journeyings as these
  Are only rivets to the chain I wear.

But shouldst thou bid me pass thy gates, and feel
  The breath of freedom upon yonder plain,
Thou knowst, sweet lady, I would suppliant kneel,
  And ask to be thy captive once again.

17 *April*, 1890

SUCCESS

SUCCESS in the world's eyes?
That 's easy done.
Success in one's own?
Can that be won?

20 November, 1890

THE CEDARS ON UNCATENA

WHERE the gray boulders lie along the shore,
The grim old cedars look across the Bay,
And to the boatman resting on his oar
They tell the story of an earlier day.

And half a century hence, when we are gone,
And other eyes than ours shall watch the changing
Bay,
The gossip breezes from the cedars lone
Will gather stories of an earlier day.

1874

A TRAPPIST MONK

UNDER THE VOW OF SILENCE, IS ALLOWED TO SPEAK
ON HIS DEATH-BED

A TRAPPIST monk lay dying
 On his pallet, at Valsainte;
There was sunshine on the windows,
 On the Alps his looks were bent.

All the beauty of the heavens
 Through the narrow casement came,
And the poor monk in his anguish
 Felt a long-forgotten flame.

He was old and pale and haggard,
 And had lived in toil and fast,
Never questioned, never faltered;
 But his hour had come at last.

Ere the long sleep, one awakening
His lips once more unsealed.
Was it thought of a life wasted
That came to him revealed?

A dream of the old mother,
And the home at eventide?
Or the fair face of the maiden
He had sought to make his bride?

His heart was beating faster
As they bent to hear his word;
But he sank back on the pillow:
" Too late!" was all they heard.

8 *January*, 1891

THE BROADSWORDS OF SCOTLAND

THERE 'S a cloud on the hill,
   And a murk in the air;
Our plaids are thrown by,
   And our broadswords are bare!

Do you hear the wild bagpipe
   Sound far o'er the pines?
Can you mark where the Saxon
   Is forming his lines?

Do you see our old chief,
   With his bonnet set down
On his brow, where the gray
   Mingles in with the brown?

Do you see his four sons
   Marching close to their sire, —
Their faces all still,
   But their bosoms on fire?

One moment to look
  As they form for the charge,
While the glint of the sun
  Falls on broadsword and targe, —

The next, one great torrent
  Pours over the brae!
Now, Southron, art ready?
  The Clans are away!

THE BROADSWORDS OF SCOTLAND

THE broadswords of Scotland
　　Are things of the past;
Their owners are now making
　　Boats that are fast.

But when they come here
　　O'er the ocean so rough,
'T is only to find
　　They are not fast enough.

18 *February*, 1891

P. S.

I CAN'T accept your offer, sir;
Indeed, I 'm not inclined
To marry anybody yet.
P. S. I 've changed my mind.

3 December, 1891.

"IN LARGE CALM HALLS."

"IN large calm halls"
   Is music flowing;
Upon the walls
   Old armor hangs;
Along the moat
Where ferns are growing,
Their green tops showing,
The white swans float.
   O maiden, tell!
   Is thy heart also calm?
Soon will that bell
The echoes charm,
And the hour proclaim
When I shall claim
Thee for my own
Till life is done.

56

Ere moonlight touches the silent river,
Or the land-breeze ruffles the swelling sea,
Thou wilt be mine, be mine forever
Now art thou ready to come with me?
  Dost fear no harm?
  Is thy heart still calm?

7 April, 1892

"IS IT A DREAM? NAY, BUT THE LACK OF IT THE DREAM."

I THOUGHT it was my lady's voice,
   And yet she is not here;
But always knows my heart's own choice
   Is only this, to have her near.

So when the doubtful ocean seems
   A stormy world between us two,
We know these distances are dreams,
   And only love is always true.

7 *April,* 1892

A BALLAD OF DOWN EAST

WHEN fishing-craft are riding high
　　To breast the combing sea,
I trow the fisher's thoughts will fly
Fast, fast through all the doubtful sky
　　To find his cottage in the lee.

In thought he sees a sweet young face
　　Look out towards the combing sea, —
The last fair flower of his race,
In whose bright eyes he sees a trace
Of her who helped him build the place,
　　The cottage by the lea.

He sees the evening fire glow,
　　So safe from storm and combing sea;
He sees her come, he sees her go,
And loves her every step to know
　　Within the cottage on the lea.

But changes come to skippers bold,
　Who steer along the combing sea;
And new things take the place of old,
And true love still will take his hold
　On hall or cottage in the lee.

So she has gone, the maiden fair,
　Whose face made bright the combing sea;
But still the skipper fishes there,
And still his thoughts will wander where
　He sees the cottage in the lee.

11 *January*, 1894

"THERE'S A BREEZE IN THE BAY"

THERE'S a breeze in the bay,
  And the low western shore
Looks hazy and gray.
  Do you hear the deep roar
Of the sea that is calling us out to the fray?

Will you come, friend, with me
  Through the night and the day,
  Far out towards the sun,
To the heart of the sea?
Where salt winds are driving,
And gray gulls are diving
  In wild ocean fun;
While lifting waves tell,
  Fly we never so fast,
The tale they know well
  Of a storm that is passed.

The sunshine we 'll meet
  As we sail through the foam,
And the whitecaps so fleet
  Be our heralds for home.

For the shore there 's a day,
  And a day for the sea;
There 's a breeze in the bay —
  Are you coming with me?

25 January, 1894

THE UNEMPLOYED

GAY brooks came laughing down the hills,
  And buds were swelling early,
While Winter, on a late snow-bank,
  Alone was looking surly,

When through a bit of swaying woods
  I loitered, somewhat dreaming,
And came upon a bluebird's song,
  So free and happy seeming.

I called the little singer down,
  And asked what he was doing.
"I'm doing nothing, — nothing now;
  Next week I shall be wooing."

8 *March*, 1894

TOUT FOITZ CHEVALIER

A SOLDIER rude no more,
    I think he would have been
Living alone for war,
    And dying in some scene
        Of battle, soon forgot, —
        Such is the soldier's lot, —

Save that one day he saw,
    When riding down the street,
Standing within her door,
    A maid so fair, so sweet,
        That all else was forgot, —
        Such is the soldier's lot.

And from that day the knight
    In the young warrior grew,
In those young eyes the light
    Had told him something new;
        Something he ne'er forgot
        Whate'er might be his lot.

12 *April*, 1894

A HEALTH — TO THE UNWISE

I DRINK to him who leaps
  Ever before he looks;
I drink to him who keeps
  Away from learned books;
    Who sings his song
    The whole day long,
Nor sees the clouds arising;
    His eye is bright,
    His heart is light,
His actions most surprising.

But though the world may chide,
  By him I take my stand,
And smiling by his side,
  And holding by his hand,
    I drink to him to-day;
    Now tell me who will say,
Whether my youth, with sunny eyes,
Is not the wisest of the wise.

9 *April*, 1894

THE GOOD FAIRY

A SLENDER dame
With quaint tall hat.
Which way she came,
Or what she's at,
You wonder, ere she's out of sight.
At all events she's something bright;
A lively step, a lively eye,
A kind sharp look, in passing by,
A slender stick within her hand, —
You wouldn't know it was a wand;
And when she's gone, you scarce know why,
Amid your days of joy and pain,
You often wish that by-and-bye
You'll see that merry face again.

4 December, 1894

WHERE WOULD YOU BE?

SOMETIMES upon a mountain high,
  Beyond the farthest tree or sod
Where foot of man has not yet trod,
To find where bluest is the sky,
With not another mortal near, —
    But to-night I would be here.

Sometimes among the white-caps gay,
Riding along the billows free,
So full of tidings from the sea,
In sunny regions of the bay,
Or plunging in its waters clear, —
    But to-night I would be here.

Sometimes in countries far away,
To read in History's varied page
The stormy tale of age on age,
To see the towers and convents grey
Built part in love and part in fear, —
    But to-night I would be here.

13 *December*, 1894

MY PET EXTRAVAGANCE

OF good big oaths — although perhaps
　　It sounds a little rough
To put it down in black and white —
　　I want to have enough!

I like to have an oath to spare,
　　An oath to give away,
An oath to lend unto a friend,
　　An oath to put away.

It makes the talking easy like,
　　And pleasant, too, to watch,
Caramba! here, Cospetto! there,
　　With damns and things to match.

And now I hope you recognize
　　How much I do forbear
When, in my daily walks and talks,
　　I never, never swear.

11 *April,* 1895

THE ORANGE BLOSSOM AND THE
FROST

WILL you tell us, gallant bird,
        Who flew so fast through storm and calm,
What message did you carry south?
        Was it a note of coming harm?
The gentle night, perhaps, had wept
        And left its tears upon the flower,
When came your wing and lightly swept
        The dewdrop in the morning hour.
And did you sing in Orange grove,
        "Alas! though I am coming back
To the bright gardens that I love,
        The stern Ice-King is on my track!"

12 *December*, 1895

REFORM

SINCE onto measures of reform
    The Game Club has been hurled,
The first thing to begin upon
    Is to reform the world.

The scenery we will not touch, —
    The general view, I mean;
But dirt itself shall disappear,
    And all the world be clean.

The mercury shall never rise
    Higher than eighty-four,
And zero shall be cold enough
    Outside of my front door.

Most of the weather shall be fine,
    With just enough of doubt
To give the world, at five o'clocks,
    Something to talk about.

We won't eliminate the fools, —
    'T would call for too much fuss;
And then they partly do amuse
    The wiser ones (that's us!).

But bores shall be no longer born;
    The living ones be sent
To pass the time in Borneo,
    Until their days are spent;
And when they die must leave a sign
    To tell which way they went.

To tell the whole long story
    Would fill up many books;
A few things only can be named: —
    We must reform the cooks,

The man who can "arrange a fire,"
    And fills our eyes with tears;
The burglar at the window-pane,
    Who causes half our fears.

And one thing more I 'll whisper:
  No matter who survives,
In certain matters of detail
  We must reform our wives.

What do I hear? — a certain sound
  Echo along the shelves?
'T is but in play, yet seems to say,
  " Better reform yourselves! "

21 *January*, 1897

IF THERE WERE DREAMS TO SELL

IF there were dreams to sell
    What would you buy?
Some cost a passing bell,
    Some a light sigh,
That shakes from Life's fresh crown
Only a roseleaf down.
        If there were dreams to sell,
        Merry and sad to tell,
        And the crier rang the bell,
            What would you buy?

A cottage lone and still,
    With bowers nigh,
Shadowy, my woes to still
    Until I die.
Such pearl from Life's fresh crown
Fain would I shake me down.
        Were dreams to have at will
        This would best heal my ill,
            This would I buy.

MEMORY

IN boyhood's time, with gay and careless mien
   We passed along life's bright and sunny ways,
Nor knew the friend that by our side, unseen,
   Went gathering pictures for our older days.

If little troubles, like a summer shower,
   Did fill our eyes with unbecoming tears,
Would Memory bring to mind a happy hour,
   And fled were all our idle woes and fears.

When on the shoulders older grown and worn
   Life's burden came, so full of care and pain,
Memory stood guard, and half the care was gone,
   For thinking of those early days again.

Has grief e'er smitten us with sudden hand,
   Till courage seemed to fail and hope to go,
Dear Memory! yes it was at thy command
   We raised our banners up and kept them so.

Around the camp, giving our post no heed,
A million sleeping sentinels you seem;
Comes the right signal,—each with lightning speed
Sounds the alarm, and wakes us from our dream.

And I shall call thee still our dearest friend;
For Love itself is mostly Memory;
The rest is Hope and Trust. Now can you mend
Those three to make a goodly company?

7 January, 1897

WRITTEN AT THE LAST MEETING

OF THE

GAME CLUB

I WAS hunting for verses to give you to-day,
But felt sure that nothing was coming my way,
Till I chanced on a paper the Lindsleys had dropped,
So I seized it, and into my pocket it popped.
Then I went to my study and copied it proud, —
If you will hold them, I will read it aloud.

The first part is his, and the rest is his wife, —
'T is clear they've writ poetry 'most of their life!
Real poetry's scarce, as most every one knows;
But enough of the preface — pray listen, here goes!

When memory beckons with its finger right,
And marshals happy scenes of long ago,
Is it too much to hope that here to-night
Another such may into memory grow?

76

From other climes we come to offer here
A little fragrance of a pleasant land;
A scent of flowers, of the coming year,
Put into verse, and all at your command.

'T is but a word, perhaps, may be a link
To bind both you and us henceforth to think
Where'er we are, this much we know alway,
The Milton friendships have come here to stay.

8 *April*, 1897

CHARADE

M_Y first is heard on shore,
    And felt at sea;
It bears me to her
    And from thee.

My second is "her,"
    And also "thee;"
The point to settle is, —
    Which shall it be?

Why my whole is my whole
    I never could say;
It's awaiting the order
    To anchor or weigh.

Unfurl the white sails;
    Let the ship wear to sea:
It shall take me to her,
    It shall take me from thee.

24 *January*, 1895

CHARADE

MY first is so bright, and my first is so gay,
  And it shines round my second through all
    the glad day,
And my whole in the first of my second so sweet
Helps to bring all the world to my second's fair feet.

22 February, 1882

CHARADE

WILL you come with me to the forest glade
    To hear the hounds in cry?
My first is seeking the deepest shade
    To shun the hunter's eye.

Will you come with me when the battle's o'er,
    And the soldier has breathed his last?
My second is bidding you weep once more,
    Once more — and all is past.

Will you come with me to the mountain stream
    Where the rocks hang grey and dank?
A bit of heaven my whole may seem,
    A tiny bit in a mossy bank.

22 *February*, 1882

CHARADE

MY first doth often bear the stamp
    That tells of love, that tells of camp,
Or brings unto my lady's chair
White roses for her bonny hair;
Or aids the squire before the fight
To hand my second to the knight.
My whole I hardly dare to name,
That is aloud, to ears polite;
But I may tell you without shame
It is the armour of the night.

WOODSTOCK, *May*, 1895

CHARADE

MY first a sort of sportive elf,
   When you were young might be yourself.
When you were young, quite young I mean,
My second on the village green
I dare to guess you often did,
Half in the twilight shadows hid.
I might suggest, if I knew how,
You may incline to do it now.
When you were young, then you and I
Were just my third, I won't say why;
But you may add this, if you will,
Despite our years we are so still.

My whole I hand you with my bow, —
It never did exist till now, —
And if you wish to hear the truth
Its whole existence is its youth.

2 *May*, 1895

CHARADE

MY first, unless your wits are dull,
    You 've seen fast followed by a bull;
My second fills the poet's page,
Or points the wisdom of the sage;
My whole is in the garden seen,
Bright gold amid the clustering green.

CHARADE

MY first is when some little boy
    Attempts without detection,
For purposes of childish joy,
    Unauthorized inspection.

My second may be said to hold
    A relative position,
Who comes upon him unawares
    And thus defeats his mission.

My whole, my saucy whole describes
    His language without measure,
When he narrates in diatribes
    His interrupted pleasure.

CHARADE

MY first and second was my third,
　　But said at once it would n't do!
In fact, before an hour was passed,
　　Declared and vowed it was n't true.
My whole repeats the tale again,
　　Neglectful of these protestations;
It also lives in plots and pain,
　　And is the terror of the nations.

CHARADE

OH, many people say they love my first,
　　Though 't is a thing they little understand;
They often think the very best the worst,
Or guess the worst is from a master hand.

The centre of the universe to me,
My next with pleasure rests on land or sea;
My third, where'er in foreign lands you tramp,
Proves the great value of the postage stamp.

To make this little riddle quite my whole
Is more than I can do to save my soul.

CHARADE

MY first two syllables might well describe
  A leaping grasshopper, a pair of tongs;
My last three tell you what is what,
And to the age of gods and myths belongs;
My whole is nothing but a fancy illustration,
Beloved by standard poets of every age and nation.

CHARADE

IN early periods of my youth
    My too indulgent first
Did strive to lead me to the Truth,
    But always feared the worst!

The facts are clearer to me now, —
    She ever did her best
To spoil me all that she knew how;
    My parents did the rest!

My second flashes through the sky,
    And lights the dimpled lake,
And if the doctors do not lie,
    Does strange impressions make.

My whole the first should never be,
    And must not be the last;
'T is something that you should not see
    Upon a day of fast.

But when you make it in a room
With a becoming bow,
'T would take a second Chesterfield
To really show you how.

February, 1896

CHARADE

MY first two, be it understood,
    Is always sweet and sometimes good.
The sage, the youth, the babe in arms,
Have all surrendered to its charms.
In many colours it is found;
I think I like it best well browned.

My next is oldest of the old
And newest of the new,
The stepping stones of history
On which the world got through.

My whole is liked by half the crowd,
And hated by the rest;
Is known by talking long and loud, —
Now is my riddle guessed?

CHARADE

MY first a member of the Arkwright Club,
  And navigator of a famous tub.
My next smacks much of China and Japan,
Is made to keep its place by the rattan.

And you may be my whole, but not too much
And you will have the merry world in touch;
But if beyond the proper law you go
The merry world will shout aloud, No! no!

CHARADE

MY first, the biggest thing on earth,
    Creates a curious emotion,
To which, if we could do my next,
    We all would live upon the ocean.

My whole is always following,
    But never overtakes,
A sort of aftermath in books,
    A finish for the cakes.

CHARADE

THE bell was rocking in the spire, —
They did my first unto the fire;
My next was speechless, but the crowd
Made use of language strong and loud;
While all they did the flames to fight
Was at my whole and aimless quite.

CHARADE

THE frosty julep, the cocktail, and such
    Good missionaries of an honest thirst,
Their virtues gain in part (but not too much)
    From the recesses of my hidden first.

My next I see around me, — yes, in scores, —
    Good, bad, indifferent, and short and tall;
The youngest, when he sees me, mostly roars.
    With all their faults, I hope I love them all.

My whole is all about us in the air,
    But most is heard of when the poets sing;
And up to date, as far as I'm aware,
    Its chief and only business is to ring.

December, 1896.

CHARADE

M^Y first is a sign of the knight
  In History's page, you may say;
My next is a source of delight
  To small boys, and relief to the grey.
My whole does assemble the wise and the bright
  All intent for to see the fools play.

June, 1897

APPENDIX

97

TRIOLET

WE walked toward the west
    (With our violet eyes).
We walked toward the west, —
You may guess all the rest, —
And 't was all for the best,
Though I say it with sighs.
We walked toward the west
(With our violet eyes).

12 *December*, 1883

To W. R. E.

I 'LL tell you a secret.
    Just hark in your ear,
Though my name must be kept in the dark,—
    'T is the high tide of Spring,
    When all the birds sing,
And the Game Club is out on a lark.

    The red tide of strawberries
        Creeps from the South,
And the snow has gone back to the sky,
    And soon the green clover
    Will blush like a lover,
Because the warm Summer is nigh.

    Then meet me, my poet,
        Beneath the tall palm,
With beating heart offer thy vows.
    No one drops from the eaves,
    And the trees take their leaves
With all of their prettiest boughs.

Ah! why that fond start?
Be silent, my heart!
For, happiness comes not to stay;
The asparagus-bed
Has heard a light tread,
And the tulips are calling " This way!"

What is this? quite a shower!
It may last an hour —
How exceedingly bad for his trouses —
If he won't take the pains
To come in when it rains
He may go back to building his houses.

14 *May*, 1884

THE PARTING MEETING OF THE GAME CLUB

WAS it not fair when Bowditch was indulging
    In devious ways (to call it nothing worse),
And came, to-night, with pocket simply bulging
    In all directions with *impromptu* verse, —

Was it not fair, a careless moment seizing,
    To steal a little morsel of that prize,
And, accidentally one pocket easing,
    To masquerade, *pro tem.*, in Bowditch guise?

Here then it is, — we'll hope he isn't vexed,
    And call it — say, his best one — till his next!

Nay? do you vote it isn't fair?
    And I must write, instead, my own Farewell?
Name any task but that, O lady fair!
    The accents would be broken ere they fell.

31 *May*, 1882

THE DOLEFUL STATE OF THE DAMNED

(WRITTEN BACK TO A FRIEND NOT YET DAMNED)

YOU said you'd like to know, when I got in
this condition,
How I liked the change of scene, and the people
who were damned.
Well! I'm writing by my window in a halo of per-
dition,
As becomes a new arrival, in this territory
crammed.

But it isn't half so bad a place as people used to
tell,
For we have some jolly devils here to mix our
lemonade;
And it's all a thing of habit, when you come to live
in Hell,
To find the climate pleasant at four hundred in
the shade.

And you see we are not tied up with a lot of old
restrictions,
All meant to save our souls from Hell, which
we 've no use for now,
And we drink our coffee daily in spite of our con-
victions;
And if we lie abed till noon, there is n't any row.

So we seem to breathe a freer air, and everything
is cheerful,
Instead of always working hard to do the things
we ought;
And the little fires round about that all supposed
so fearful,
Are really quite engaging, which no one would
have thought.

And then we summer boarders here are not allowed
to grumble,
And all the time is playtime, for there is n't any
work;

So all the toils of years gone by seem but a perfect
jumble,
While the lexicon of Hell, 't is clear, needs no
such word as *shirk*.

We just got on the roof and looked across a fence
neglected
To Paradise, where all the good have gone to live
in bliss;
But we found the people looked so very bored and
so dejected,
That all of us agreed that that was no such place
as this.

My brimstone bath is ready now, so I must say
farewell!
I'll send this letter out inscribed upon a fire-
brick.
It is n't quite within the rules to send out notes
from Hell;
So you must keep it shady. Good-bye. Your
loving Dick.

31 *March*, 1886

LETTER TO THE GAME CLUB
FROM BATH.

NOT yours alone the tears that fell
    While widening waters hid from sight
The hills, the shores we knew so well,
    As evening faded into night.
We could not our emotion hide,
    To see those shores receding far;
Our tears in torrents filled the tide,
    And helped the ship across the bar.

A week of snow and wintry breeze,
    And then our hearts began to swell,
As, lifting with the lifting seas,
    We heard fair Biddy's welcoming yell,
While poised upon the Fastnet rocks
    She seemed to counterfeit the bees.

And one there was who sought to land,
  Until they bound him to the mast,
And filled his ears with scouring sand —
  Alas, that fairy vision passed!

England we found all buried up:
  An inch of snow had somehow dropped.
The railroads were half paralyzed,
  And traffic everywhere was stopped.
And so we left the London fog
  And welcomed France's milder showers;
We reached, we passed the snow-crowned Alps,
  To seek fair Italy's promised flowers.

Milan Cathedral! yes, we love it well.
  Its clustered columns and majestic aisles
Far more the solemn story tell
  Than paltry words: and where it smiles
With glorious sunshine streaming down the nave,
  A path to heaven it almost seems to pave.

To Genoa on! for, Time with mocking laugh
  Cracks his rude whip and urges on the day.
No patient pilgrim he, with scrip and staff, —
  At railroad speed he makes his conquering way.
O mighty Time, the world is at your feet,
  The moments crumble at your lightning touch.

Oh, let us but this happy hour repeat!
  Time irresponsive cries, "You ask too much,"
And so to Genoa, while the Apennine
  Still bears a gleaming helmet on its brow,
Though foaming torrents by the sombre pine
  Bring icy tidings from the yielding snow.

The sky was shining, though the sea was rough,
  As near we came and heard the breakers' roar,
And Genoa! Genoa could not smile enough
  To see us coming to its curving shore.
But Genoa, not thy chattering market-place,
  Nor sunny villas set in gardens gay,
Could long detain us, in our rapid pace,
  As on to Royal Rome we made our way.

Rome, Florence, Venice — Ah! such themes as these,
  No hasty traveller's pen may dare essay;
So pass we back to England, if you please,
  Stopping a week in Paris by the way;
A week in Paris just to steady it,
  And help Carnot to hold his place awhile —
The Bonnet? yes, they had to make it fit, —
  I know you 'll like it, nothing there but style!

And finally we came to Bath; and here
Repentant Britons congregate each year,
And pay with faces the reverse of merry,
A hundred times again for every quart of sherry, —
Of heavy Burgundy, or Spanish sherry;
Of rich Madeira, or of rare old Port.
Your correspondent too, they do immerse
In tanks of water up to ninety-nine,
While doctors order him, to make it worse,
To give up sugar, pastry, cheese, and wine.
And then a ruffian comes and seizes him
(One much confused in consonants and vowels),
And swiftly muffles each rheumatic limb

In a big ambuscade of red-hot towels.
They pack him where he cannot reach the bell,
And then retire, turning fast the key,
And in this sort of ante-mortem Hell
He counts much on the Game Club's sympathy.
What's left of him will come to Boston soon,
I hope before you see the July moon.
Farewell, I've given you quite too much verse,
And writing makes the rheumatism worse.

23 *May*, 1888

NEW POEMS TO OLD TITLES

"TELL me, my heart, if this be love;"
  I can't at all make out.
I find it difficult to move,
  And feared it was the gout.

Then think it over well, my heart,
  For I am growing stout,
I.never yet have been in love,
  I often have the gout.

Then know, my heart, if this be love,
  If there's no room for doubt,
I swear by all the gods above
  I'd rather have the gout.

7 *January*, 1885

NEW YEAR'S VERSES
To E. W. E.

HERE'S a book that tells about our Philip's
machinations.
When Uncle Sam had called the nation's boys
out to defend her,
They rode, they walked, they grumbled, fought and
lived on scanty rations,
And they all know where Sheridan was on the
day of Lee's Surrender.

The Rebels marched by day and night, and every
morn they swore,
By all the boots they ever had, their chance was
getting slender.
They fought and fasted till each man could fast
and fight no more,
And the Rebels know where Sheridan was on the
day of Lee's Surrender.

112

It happened on an April day, when the grass be-
   neath was springing,
   And all the buds on all the trees above were
   growing tender, —
But read the book and you shall know when your
   Sabbath bells were ringing,
   In Yankee land, where Sheridan was on the day
   of Lee's Surrender.

1 *January*, 1867

To E. W. E.

With Holden's Dissector.

I AM offering Edward a dangerous book
  Which one hardly dares to look twice at.
When he 's read it all through, with its horrible cuts,
  We ne'er shall know what he may slice at!

Take the knives from the table! quick, somebody do!
  He 's looking about for the baby!
Do you think he could do her much harm with a
    fork?
  Now pray be content with a tabby!

I shall say to my wife when he comes here to call
  (Which I think proves I 'm not quite a noddy)
What I said when the mad bull jumped over the
    wall,—
  " He shall reach *me* but over your body!"

1869

To RALPH

PLAY, my boy, the hours go swift,
    And the sun shines bright to-day;
Play while there's one to give you a lift,
    For the sun shines bright to-day.

Weep, my little boy, weep no more,
    Brief is your little sorrow;
Plenty of play for my boy to-day,
    But none of us know to-morrow.

1869

To EDITH

HAPPY Birdie, are you there too?
　　Brave little head and bonny eyes!
And have you learned in months so few
　　How to ask for a New Year's prize?

Here it is, with a New Year's kiss,—
　　Go and try it, my Birdie,—
A walnut chair for our little miss,
　　And one for Ralph the sturdy.

1869

To E. E. F.

(WITH PAINTS, PALLET, AND BRUSHES)

WHEN the South wind so gay
  Comes over the sea,
And beyond Buzzard's Bay
  The summer is free,

On our favorite shore
  We will gather once more,
And the slumbering waters
  Shall wake to the oar.

Oh, the blue wave may curl,
  But shall yield up its hue,
And the landscape surrender
  Hill and valley to you.

Short time the wild rose
  On the Island hill grows,
Yet your canvas will hold
  All its bloom ere it goes.

To E. W. E.

"O DOCTOR, wilt thou leave town to-night?
　　And what would you do, if you were me?
My child dropped a pail on his finger-nail
　　And he's sure to ask for thee."

"If I were alone with that boy to-night,
　　And he were alone with me,
My hand should be on a shingle light,
　　And that boy upon my knee."

He has plastered a hundred milk-white boys,
　　He has blue-pilled a hundred black,
And he's off to try for New Year's toys
　　With the north wind at his back.

But when he rode up to the Milton Hall,
　　"What news from the West?" axed we.
"The town is all quiet, the children on diet,
　　And I'm come to bide a wee."

1 *January*, 1882

To RALPH

DOWN in the meadow the chanting quail
  Echoes his mate on the hill,
In the cedar-tree by the broken rail
  The hawk is watching still.

But a footstep light and an eye so bright
  Are nearing the breezy hill,—
Now hawk and quail say a long good-night,
  Your voices shall soon be still.

1 *January*, 1882

119

TO ELLEN

(WITH A SILVER BUTTERFLY PIN)

"LAZILY floating on a July breeze,
   Touching the flowers with a careless wing
I found the brook deep hidden in the ferns,
   And hovered there awhile to hear it sing.

The song was sweet, and fast the time ran by,
   Till a rude gust bent all the grasses low,
And my faint struggles quickly overcome,
   Into the little torrent did I go.

Fast to a slender reed long while I clung,
   At length was fain to yield me up to death;
The summer passed while still the song was sung,
   Till winter reached the brook with icy breath."

And now the frozen butterfly and reed,
Holding thy scarf beneath a silvery wing,
When once again the summer breezes blow,
Bending above the brook, shall hear the waters
sing.

1884